How to Train the
PERFECT
PARENTS

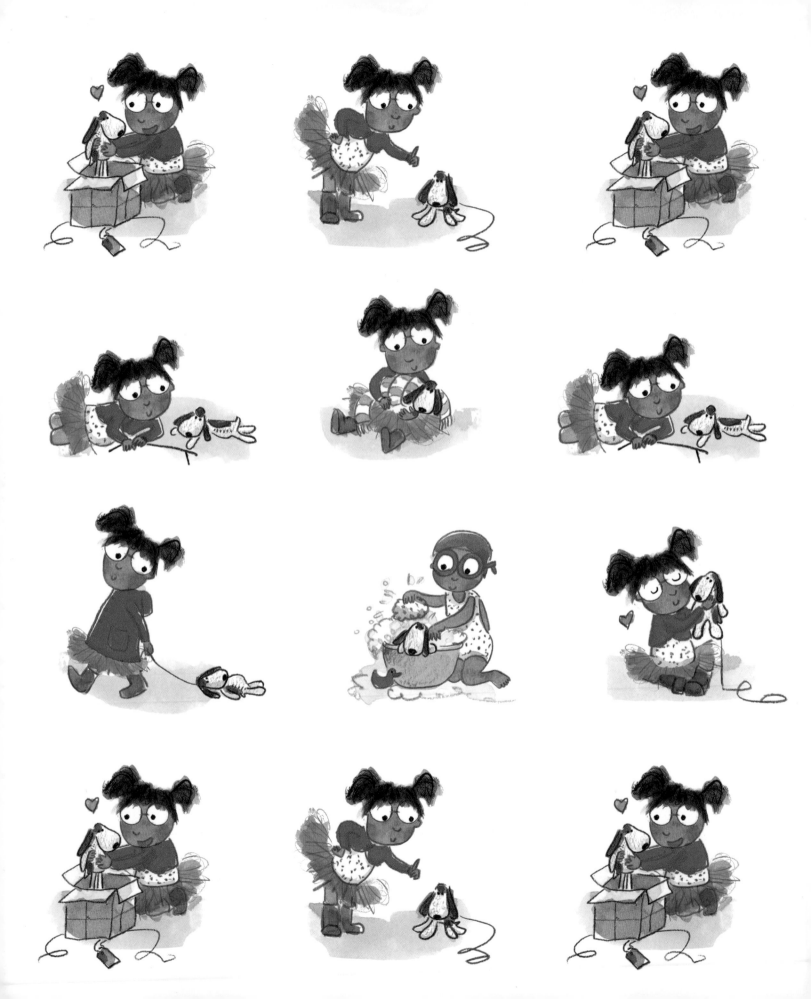

For Tate and Rufus, my perfect children.
Well, almost perfect!

A TEMPLAR BOOK

First published in the UK in 2018 by Templar Publishing,
an imprint of Kings Road Publishing, part of the Bonnier Publishing Group,
The Plaza, 535 King's Road, London, SW10 0SZ
www.bonnierpublishing.com

1 3 5 7 9 10 8 6 4 2

ISBN 978-1-78370-833-8

This book was typeset in Futura and Shoebox

Designed by Genevieve Webster and Helen Chapman
Edited by Isobel Boston and Katie Haworth

Printed in China

How to Train the
PERFECT
PARENTS

Rebecca Ashdown

templar
books

You can **always** spot a parent.

I bet yours look a bit like this.

Parents **really** don't understand how hard it is being a kid. But, actually, being a parent can be tricky too.

Parents just don't understand what us kids want . . .

. . . and **need**.

You can't blame them. It's because they've never been trained.

Do **YOUR** parents need training?

If so, I can help . . .

With **THIS!**

My **THREE-STEP PLAN.**
My name is Mimi Lee and if you follow my *expert* advice,
your whole life will be transformed. **FOREVER!**

Step 1: Communication

Make sure you understand each other right from the start.
Clearly show your parents when you **don't** like something . . .

. . . and when you **do**.

You should practise this in the mirror.

The perfect parent will recognise **all** of these expressions.

HMMM

HOORAY!

GRRR

GASP!

UM...

YUCK!

WAH!

EEEK!

STEP 2: TRUST

You trust your parents, don't you? But do they really trust you? Prove just how responsible you can be.

A trusting parent should be able to ignore little accidents.
When they do, give them lots of treats and attention.

STEP 3: ROUTINE

Stick to a routine and be persistent. They'll soon learn.
You may have to repeat things again . . .

and again . . .

and again . . .

and again . . .

AND AGAIN.

RESULTS

How's it all going? During those quiet moments, when everyone's asleep, keep track of your progress.

The Big Push

Now you've mastered the first three steps, it's time to focus on your final goal. I call this **THE BIG PUSH.**

You'll soon know if your training has been successful.

Mine has been **very** successful.
HOORAY!

I'm going to be the BEST PUPPY PARENT ever!

As you can see, all that training has **definitely** changed my life.

I've learnt all
sorts of skills . . .

Woof! Woof! Woof!

Like my **THREE-STEP PLAN!**
That *never* fails.

STEP 1: COMMUNICATION

Make sure you understand each other right from the start.

STEP 2: TRUST

It's important to show that you are trusting.

A trusting parent should be able to ignore little accidents.

STEP 3: Routine

Stick to a routine and be persistent. They'll soon learn.

RESULTS

How's it all going? During those quiet moments,
keep track of your progress.

The Big Push

Now you've (almost) mastered the first three steps,
it's time for **THE BIG PUSH!**

You'll soon know if your training has been successful.

I **think** mine has been successful.

Although sometimes . . .

. . . the results . . .

. . . are not . . .

. . . exactly . . .

. . . what you hoped for.

MOST OBEDIENT DOG

BEST GROOMED DOG

EXIT

If things don't go to plan, go back to the drawing board and make a few changes.

Actually, well-trained parents can be quite good at helping.

Just give them a chance.

They'll soon get the hang of it.

And eventually **everything** will be perfect.

Ready, Mimi?

Wait!

Well, *almost* perfect.

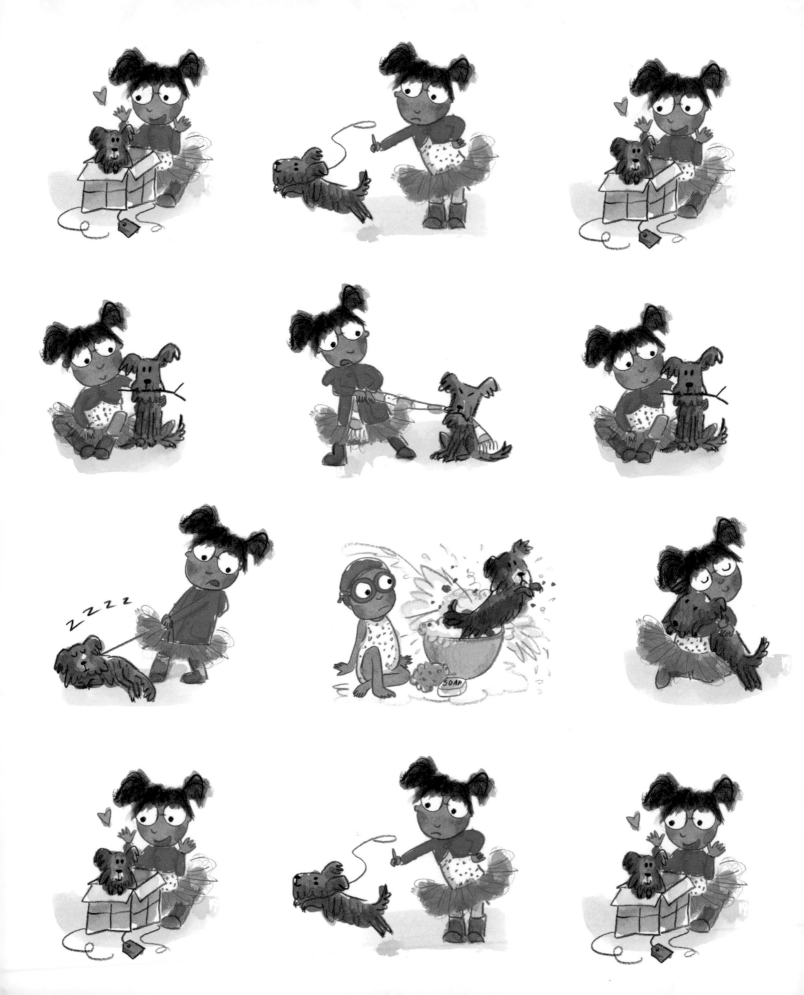